This book belongs to:

....

For Jake, with love and thanks
Anne Fine

For Ivy and Mike
Kerry Hyndman

LET IT SNOW!
is a DAVID FICKLING BOOK
published in partnership with WAITROSE

First published in Great Britain in 2017 by David Fickling Books,
31 Beaumont Street, Oxford, OX1 2NP   www.davidficklingbooks.com

Let It Snow! was inspired by the Waitrose Christmas television advertisement, 2017
Text © Anne Fine, 2017 Illustrations © Kerry Hyndman, 2017

978 191 020080 3

1 3 5 7 9 10 8 6 4 2

The right of Anne Fine and Kerry Hyndman to be identified as the author and illustrator of
this work has been asserted in accordance with the Copyright, Designs and Patents Act 1988.

WARNING: This book will fill you with festive fun!

Papers used by David Fickling Books are from well-managed forests and other responsible sources.

FSC
www.fsc.org
MIX
Paper from
responsible sources
FSC® C023419

DAVID FICKLING BOOKS Reg. No. 8340307
A CIP catalogue record for this book is available from the British Library

Edited by Alice Corrie and designed by Ness Wood

Printed and bound in Italy by L.E.G.O. S.p.A

ANNE FINE

LET IT SNOW!

*illustrated by Kerry **Hyndman***

DAVID FICKLING BOOKS

Waitrose

The Squirrels lived in a very old house. They grew loads and loads of wonderful things in their garden. Almost every day they took some to be sold in the big supermarket in town. In summer, their truck overflowed with fruit and flowers. In winter, it was stuffed with bags of vegetables.

It's Christmas Eve! If it snows, we might not get back tonight.

The Hares lived in a very new house. Every week they went shopping in their sleek car to fill a giant hamper with all sorts of delicious food and special treats.

SNOW! SNOW!
And it's falling fast!

I'll take one present each,
just in case.

After their shopping trip, the Hares were in a great hurry to get home to cook their special Christmas Eve lunch. They overtook the Squirrels' truck so fast, they nearly forced it off the road.

"That's horribly rude!" said Sam.
   "I expect they're really worried about getting back," said Mr Squirrel. "A truck like ours can drive through deep snow more easily than a car like theirs."

But when they drove round the corner . . .

. . . the Squirrels saw that the Hares' car was almost completely buried in a snowdrift.

Oh, my golly! Look at that!

It serves them right.

We'll have to help them.

Mr Squirrel got out of the truck.

"You can't stay here," he told the Hares. "It's not safe."

"Come with us," said Mrs Squirrel. "Jump in."

Harriet climbed in beside Sam. She found a dried-up parsnip on her seat and wrinkled her nose. Sam thought she was being very silly.

"We should have left you there to freeze," he hissed at her. "Then your whole family might have learned some manners."

"You can't learn manners from someone who wants to leave you to freeze!" Harriet snapped back.

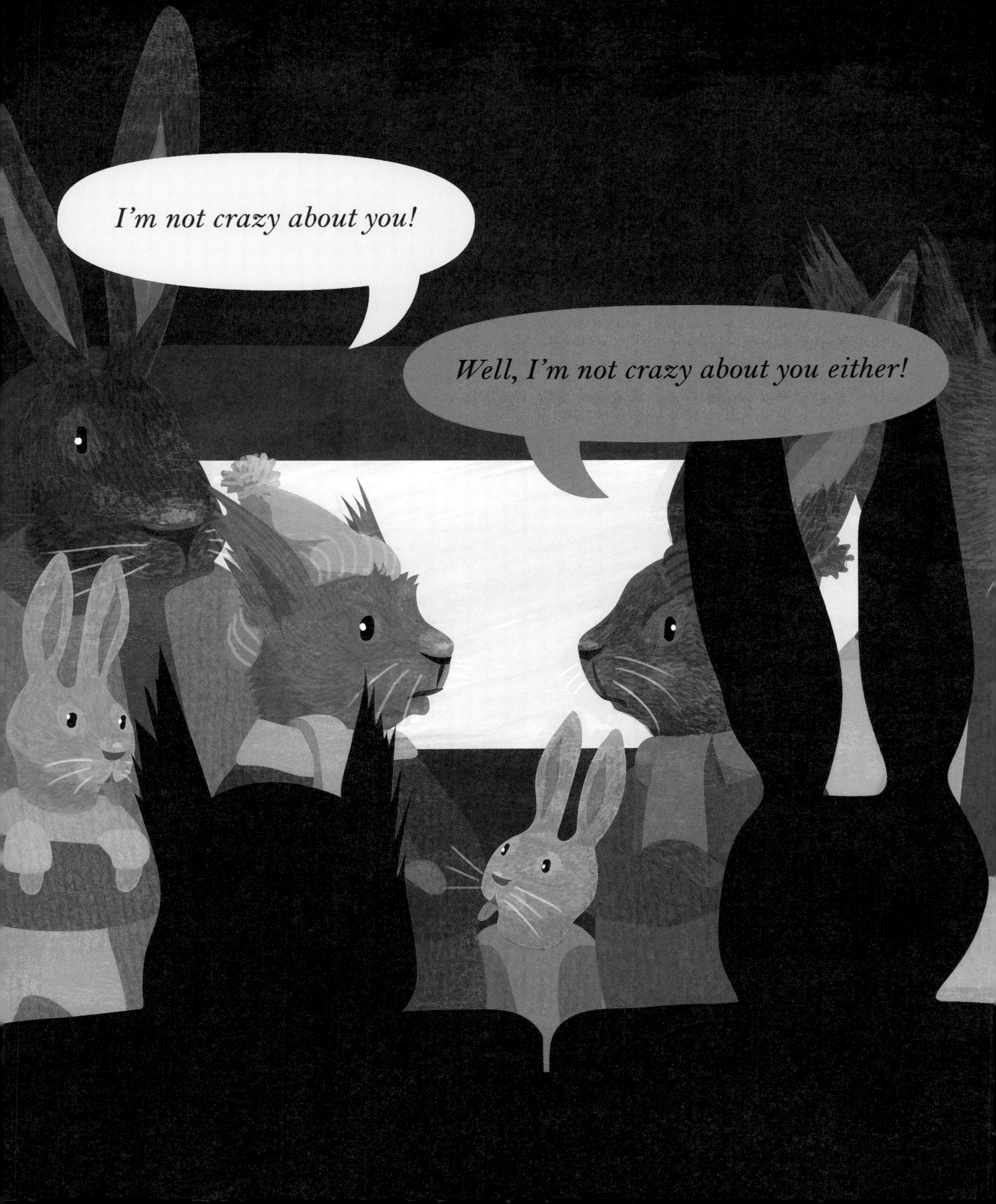
I'm not crazy about you!
Well, I'm not crazy about you either!

The snow was even deeper round the bend.
"Now we are *really* in trouble!" said Mrs Squirrel.
"Even our truck can't make its way through this."

"What a horrible way to spend Christmas Eve!" said Mrs Hare.
"Disaster!" agreed Mr Hare.

But Mr Squirrel was pointing at a wisp of smoke above
the nearby hill.
"Look!" he said. "Maybe we're in luck."

"I'm not leaving *my* Christmas present on the truck,"
said Sam.

   "If he's taking his along with him," said Harriet,
"I'm going to take *ours* too!"

There was only one table left, beside the fire.
"Bit of a squash," Mr Hare said.
"Never mind," said Mrs Squirrel. "Makes it more cosy."
The children sat on stools. *Nobody* noticed when the hare twins
started shunting the presents round and round in circles.
And *nobody* noticed what they were doing with the labels . . .

After a while, everyone was getting very hungry.

"I know," said Mr Hare. "We'll bring in our hamper full of delicious treats."

"And we'll bring some of our lovely fresh home-grown vegetables," said Mrs Squirrel.

"Yes!" everyone agreed. "Let's have a Christmas feast!"

The Christmas feast was wonderful. Even Harriet and Sam cheered up because they knew that after they'd finished, each of them would be allowed to open their very first present.

Fizz!

Pop!

Hic!

Yum!

Would you care for my Brussels sprouts, Harriet?

"Just a minute!" said Mrs Hare. "I think that gift was for Ha—"

"Hang on!" said Mr Squirrel. "Those gardening tools were meant for S—"

But Harriet and Sam weren't listening. They were delighted with their presents.

Yay!

Brrm!

"This lamp's so cheery!" Sam told everyone. "It'll brighten up our whole house!"

"Fabulous!" said Harriet. "Now I can grow flowers all around our front door!"

Everyone was so busy admiring the presents that only the twins noticed the magical trail of silvery sparks showering down from the sky to melt the snow along the road.

Not very much later, a farmer poked her head around the door.

Road's clear.

Merry Christmas!

Everyone went off, waving and happy.

"Will you come round and see my lovely front garden when it's done?" Harriet asked Sam.

"Only if you'll come and see my new shining, magic house," said Sam.

And so, next spring, the families
went to visit one another.

The Squirrels' house was filled with lovely lamplight and the Hares' front garden was bright with flowers. Everyone was happy.

RECIPE

GINGERBREAD RUDOLPHS

You will need:

125g butter

100g dark brown muscovado sugar

4 tbsp golden syrup

325g plain flour

1 tsp bicarbonate of soda

2 tsp ground ginger

Writing icing to decorate

What you need to do:

1. Preheat the oven to 170°C/gas mark 3

2. Melt the butter, sugar and syrup together in a pan, then remove from the heat

3. Sieve in the plain flour with bicarbonate of soda and ground ginger and stir in to make a stiff dough

4. Roll out on a lightly floured surface to 5mm thick

5. Cut out about 20 gingerbread Rudolphs or men and bake on lined baking trays for 10 minutes, until golden

6. Cool, then use the icing to add eyes, nose and mouth

For every book sold, a donation of 50p is made to The Trussell Trust, an anti-poverty charity which runs a network of over 400 foodbanks, giving emergency food and support to people in crisis across the UK.

the trussell trust
Stop UK Hunger